KU-876-934

FRUIT LANE

written by Pauline Mackay   illustrated by Shelley Buckner

ABLEKIDS PRESS

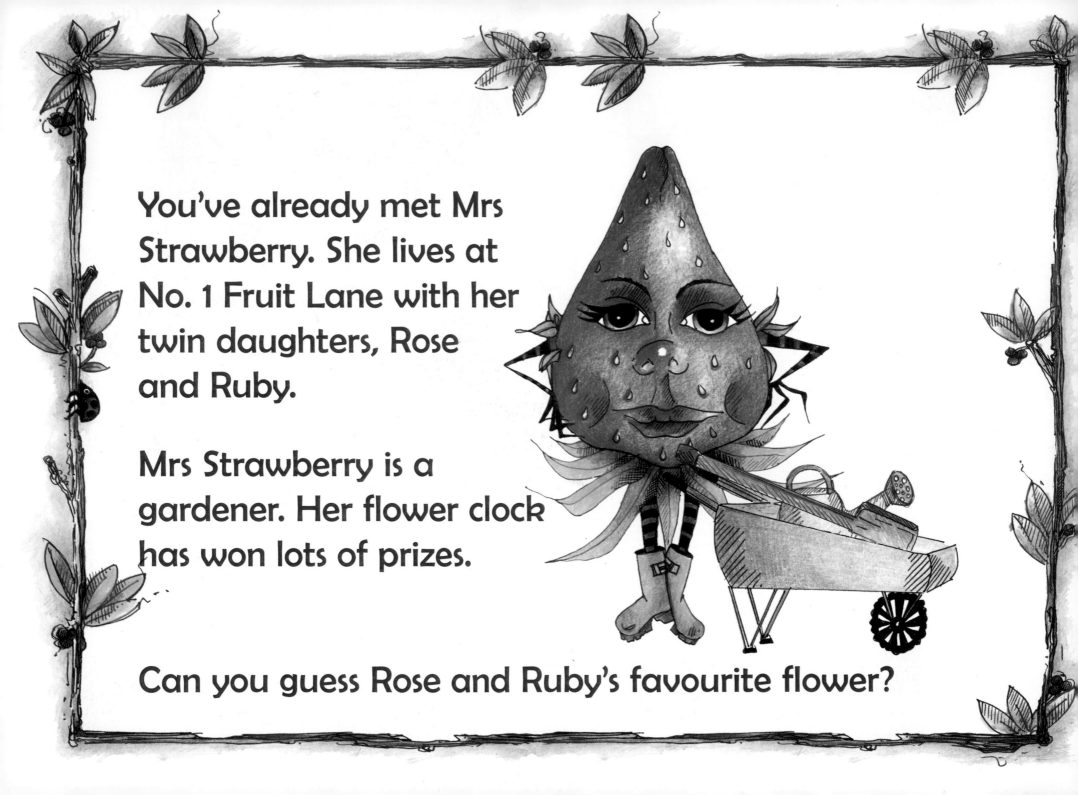

You've already met Mrs Strawberry. She lives at No. 1 Fruit Lane with her twin daughters, Rose and Ruby.

Mrs Strawberry is a gardener. Her flower clock has won lots of prizes.

Can you guess Rose and Ruby's favourite flower?

Mrs Blackberry delivers letters to all the houses in Vitamin Village.

She has to get up early in the morning to go to work, so Grandma Blackberry looks after baby Lucy.

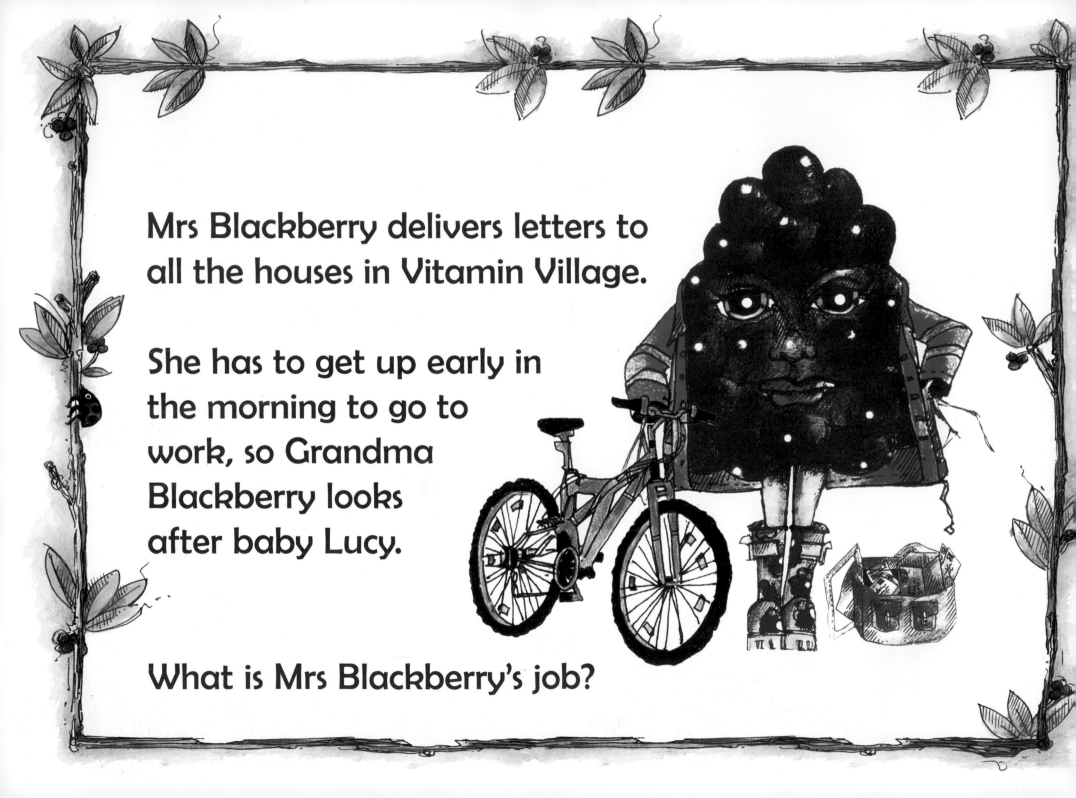

What is Mrs Blackberry's job?

Mr Orange is very proud of his new house.

His son, Neville and Ruff the dog are always in trouble for making a mess. They leave muddy footprints and puddles of water everywhere!

Who do you think built Mr Orange's house?

Miss Blueberry shares her little house at No. 4 Fruit Lane with her beloved cat, Princess.

Miss Blueberry is a hairdresser in Rapunzel's Salon in Vitamin Village square.

Can you guess her favourite shape?

Mrs Apple travels around the world taking lots of photographs of people and places and things. Sometimes her photographs are in newspapers and magazines.

Mrs Apple really likes to get home to Island House. The first thing she does is count the fish in her pond.

Can you guess why?

Miss Date loves to sparkle. She owns 'The Little Gem' jewellery shop in Vitamin Village's clock tower.

She lives next door to her best friend, Miss Blueberry.

Miss Date doesn't like mud or dirt which can be a bit of a problem living in Fruit Lane.

What is Miss Date's favourite gem?

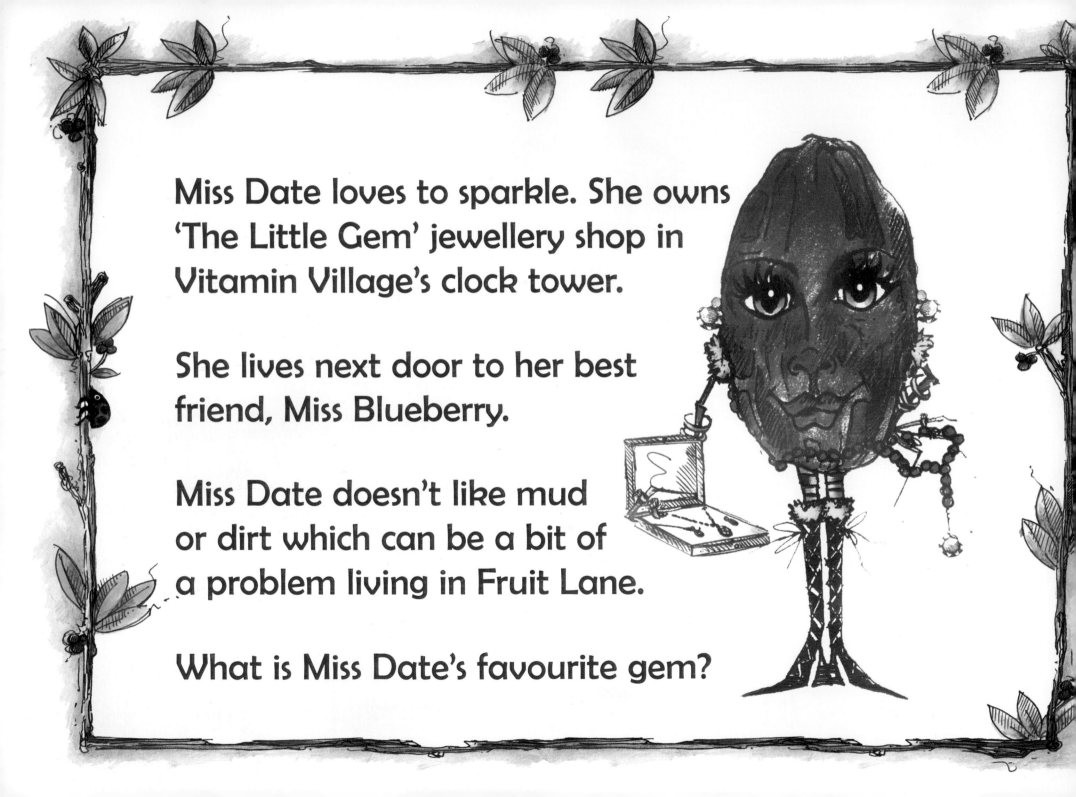

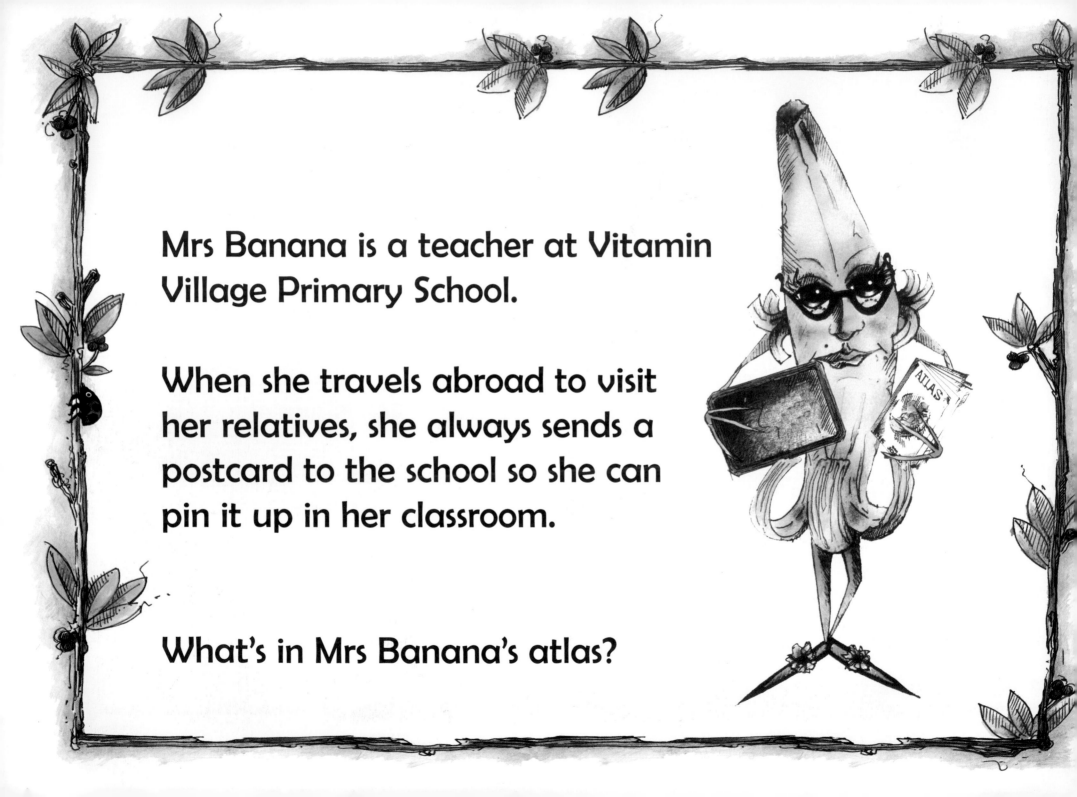

Mrs Banana is a teacher at Vitamin Village Primary School.

When she travels abroad to visit her relatives, she always sends a postcard to the school so she can pin it up in her classroom.

What's in Mrs Banana's atlas?

Mr Grapefruit is a chef at The Eatwell Hotel so it's not surprising that he lives in Mushroom Wood House in Fruit Lane.

Mr Grapefruit keeps hens and geese. He likes nothing better than a fresh egg for his breakfast.

Which is bigger – a hen's egg or a goose's egg?

Dr Pear spends most of her time taking care of sick children at The Hospital.

When she gets home to Fruit Lane, Dr Pear enjoys looking after her bees.

Do you know what food bees make?

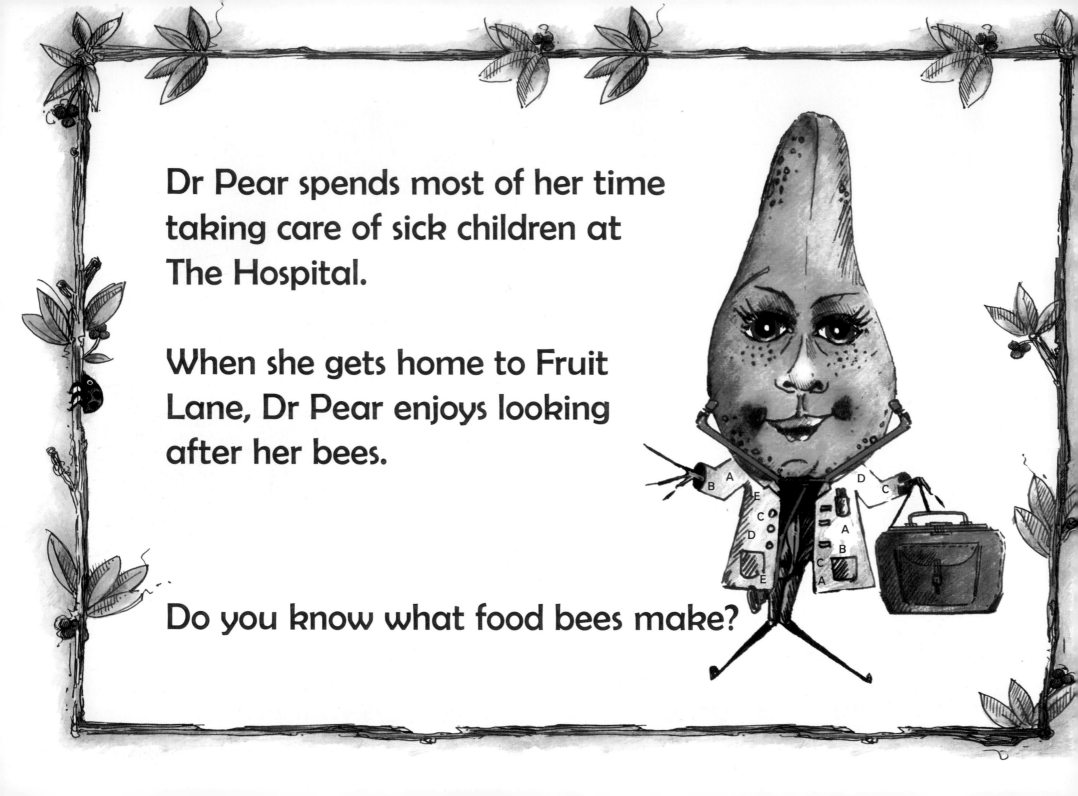

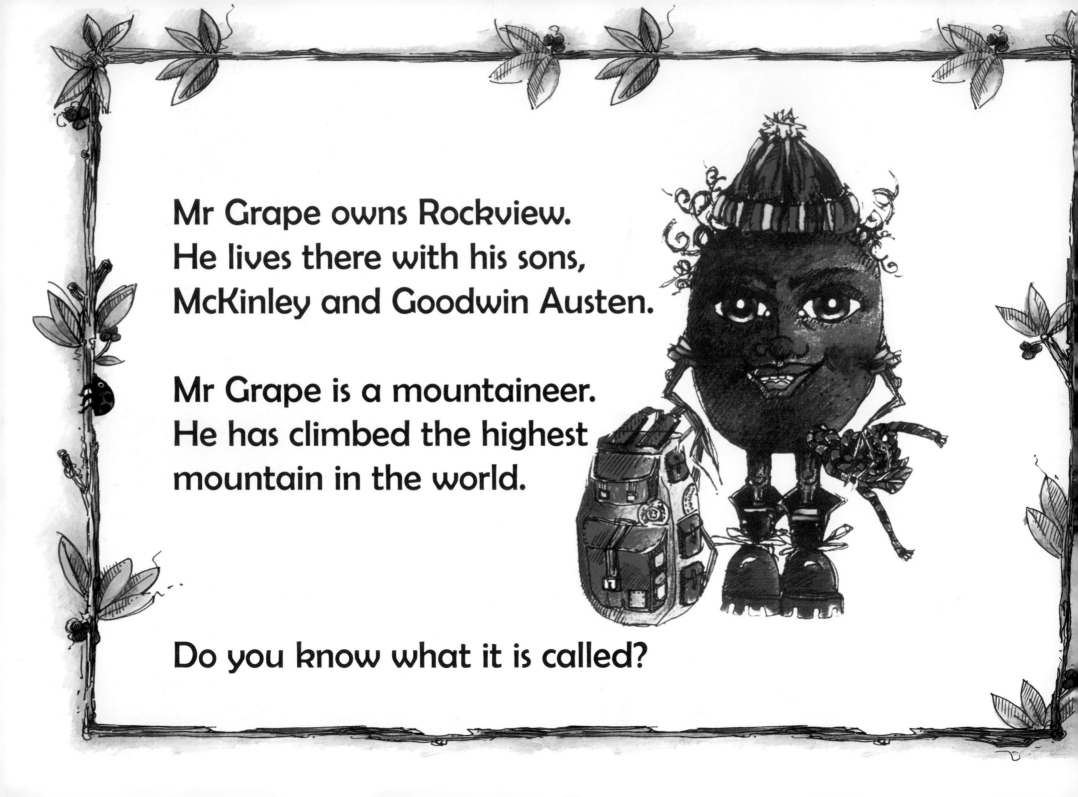

Mr Grape owns Rockview.
He lives there with his sons,
McKinley and Goodwin Austen.

Mr Grape is a mountaineer.
He has climbed the highest
mountain in the world.

Do you know what it is called?